HARRY, THE FAT BEAR SPY

HARRY, THE FAT BEAR SPY

written and illustrated
by Gahan
Wilson

Charles Scribner's Sons   New York

To Helen Schwake

Contents

HARRY, THE
FAT BEAR SPY

one The Spy Master

Harry, the fat bear, worked as a spy for his native country, Bearmania. It was not an easy job, and many times Harry wished he had another. Often he dreamed for hours on end of being a chef in some nice kitchen where he would have nothing to do all day long but prepare delicious dinners from which he could take little nibbles now and then.

But a spy Harry was, and a spy's work he must do, and when the Spy Master called Harry to Spy Headquarters, Harry went. Even though he was in the middle of a good book, and it was raining, and he had to walk through puddles and get splashed on by water thrown from passing cars, he went.

Spy Headquarters, like everything else in the spy business, pretended to be something it wasn't. Spy Headquarters pretended to be a noodle factory, and every time Harry went into it he thought to himself, "This can't be fooling anybody."

For one thing, there was always a long line of spies

standing outside of the Spy Headquarters, gossiping or waiting for assignments, and Harry was sure bears would notice and say to one another, "Listen, you can't tell me that a place with all those spies standing around outside of it hasn't got something to do with spies!"

For another thing, in order to get into the Spy Headquarters, noodle factory, you had to go through a complicated series of signals and countersignals, and Harry was absolutely certain that even though the signals and countersignals *were* changed every Wednesday, bears would notice them and nudge each other and say, "Look, you can't kid me. Those are spies, there, trying to get into a spy headquarters! I don't care what anybody says!"

Harry walked up to the bear at the door of Spy Headquarters and gave the first signal: "It certainly is hot for being around Christmastime."

The bear, who was pretending to roll a noodle, and who had been pretending to roll the same noodle all day long, gave the second signal: "Yes, but that's what happens when you make a goose wear a straw hat."

Then Harry gave the third signal, which was to recite a famous section of a poem written by one of Bearmania's leading poets:

"It certainly is hot for being around Christmastime."

You're better than Pennsylvania, Bearmania.
You're better than Transylvania, Bearmania.
You're better than any of those places.

The poem finished the countersignal and the bear pretending to roll the noodle let Harry in to the outer room of the Spy Headquarters. Harry was always embarrassed by the outer room because it was just too small and poorly equipped to make a convincing noodle factory.

"You couldn't make enough noodles for one bowl of soup in this place," thought Harry.

He went through the rear door of the room and down a long, narrow corridor; and then he knocked on a big, metal door with a microphone on one side of it and a speaker mounted over its top.

"Yes?" said a voice from the speaker.

Harry leaned over the microphone and spoke slowly and carefully into it. He knew that the microphone was faulty and if you did not put your lips directly in front of it and pronounce your words very clearly, the microphone wouldn't transmit.

"It's me, Agent Three Five Zero small case *b*," said Harry slowly and carefully.

"Who?" said the voice from the speaker over the door.

"It's me, Agent Three Five Zero small case b," repeated Harry, his voice rising.

"I'm sorry," said the voice from the speaker over the door, "I still didn't get you."

"You have to get this microphone fixed!" shouted Harry.

"I know I do," said the voice. "Don't nag."

There was a pause and then the door opened and a small, thin bear with thick glasses and a fez looked out at Harry. It was the Spy Master.

"Oh," said the Spy Master, "it's you. Come in. Come in."

He turned and went back into his office with Harry following after.

"Be sure to close the door," said the Spy Master, settling himself behind his desk. "It can stop a tank if it's closed, but it's no good at all if it's open."

Harry closed the door and tried to slide the huge bolt which was fixed to the door's inside. But the bolt was stuck and Harry couldn't get it to budge no matter how hard he tugged.

"Oh," said the Spy Master, "it's you. Come in. Come in."

"Never mind that," said the Spy Master, impatiently. "It has to be oiled, or something."

"This door isn't going to stop any tank if you don't bolt it," said Harry.

"I didn't call you to Spy Headquarters to talk about bolts," snapped the Spy Master. "I called you here to talk about something important!"

He reached over to the right side of his desk and pulled too hard at the knob of a drawer so that the entire drawer came out and all of its contents spilled in a heap on the floor. Harry offered to help, but the Spy Master waved him back.

"I'll do it myself," he said, gritting his teeth.

The Spy Master got on his hands and knees beside the pile of documents and folders and started to go through them, shaking his head and muttering. Harry knew from long experience that it was important not to get the Spy Master more upset than he happened to be at any particular moment, because it would make the Spy Master repeat himself, and things could go on for hours. So Harry just sat back, looking calm, and saying nothing.

As the Spy Master sorted through the mounds of papers on the floor, Harry noticed that a brightly colored map seemed to be giving him a good deal of trouble. It was big and floppy and the Spy Master kept getting tangled up in it like a man lost in a folding screen. The map finally wrapped itself completely around the little

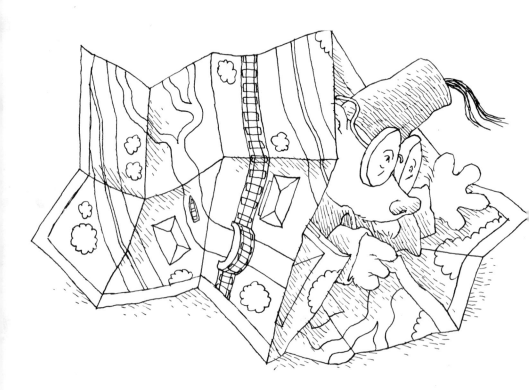

A brightly colored map seemed to be
giving him a good deal of trouble.

bear, but then he came into view again with a trium-
phant smile on his face.

"I found it," the Spy Master cried happily, and
climbing over the map's edge, he dragged it along behind him and carefully spread it out over the top of his
desk. He studied the map thoughtfully for several long
minutes, his face growing more and more perplexed.
Then, with a sigh of relief, he placed his claw firmly
near the northern edge of the map.

"This, Agent Three Five Zero small case *b,* is where
you are going. Or, rather, this is only a map, but it rep-
resents where you are going. And where you are going
is our famous, unsurpassed, National Macaroon Factory!"

Harry's eyes lit up and his stomach rumbled, for
Harry liked nothing better than macaroons. He always
kept a good supply of macaroons on his person. As if to
underline the point, Harry pulled out a macaroon, then
and there, and began to chew on it.

two Harry's Arrival

When the train slowed down and the conductor began calling, "National Macaroon Factory! Have your papers ready!" Harry began looking through his pockets for the identification which the Spy Master had given him. The identification said that Harry was a macaroon batter mixer, grade two. Of course, it wasn't true. Harry didn't have the slightest idea of how to go about mixing macaroon batter, but in the spy business you almost always go around with false identification. It is convenient, and it is expected of you.

The only trouble was, Harry couldn't seem to locate the false identification. He had no trouble finding his

Harry began looking through his pockets.

real identification, the one that said he was a spy, but, search as he would—and he went through every pocket and fold in his clothing—he couldn't find a trace of the false identification which said he was a macaroon batter mixer, grade two. The train got closer and closer to the checkpoint for the National Macaroon Factory, and Harry began to sweat a little under his cloak and slouch hat.

Suddenly, just as the train drew to a stop and the uniformed security guard entered the car, Harry remembered where he had last seen the false identification. It had been lying on the top of his bureau, in his bedroom, next to his wallet and his key ring. Harry could remember, just as clear as anything, picking up his wallet and his key ring, and putting the wallet in his left hip pocket, and the key ring in his right front pocket; but he could not remember putting the false identification anywhere. He could only remember leaving it on the top of the bureau in his bedroom.

"Identification papers, please," said the security guard, holding his hand out toward Harry and looking a little bored. Harry softly cleared his throat.

"I wonder," he whispered, "if we could have a few words in private?"

"What's that?" asked the security guard in a loud, carrying tone. "I didn't quite get you!"

Several bears in the car turned to stare curiously at them. Harry cleared his throat again and leaned a little closer to the security guard, who backed away.

"I said, 'I wonder if we could have a few words in private?'" whispered Harry. "You know—just by ourselves?"

By now all conversation in the car had stopped and all the bears were listening carefully to everything Harry and the security guard said.

"Have you got identification papers or don't you, fat bear," said the security guard, frowning. "That's all I want to know."

Realizing his situation was hopeless, Harry took out his authentic identification papers, the ones which said right out he was a spy, and handed them over to the security guard, who, for the first time since Harry had met him, smiled.

"That's more like it, chum," he said, writing "SPY" in big, red letters on a round badge and pinning the badge to the front of Harry's cloak.

Harry looked down at the badge in dismay. Having a badge with "SPY" written on it and pinned to the front

"That's more like it, chum."

of his cloak would be a terrible inconvenience.

"I wish you hadn't done this," Harry said to the security guard. "It's really going to slow me down."

"What's so special about you, chum? Why shouldn't you wear a badge?"

Then Harry saw that all the other bears had badges pinned to their fronts too, and that their badges also described their occupations. One of the bears wore a badge saying MACAROON BATTER MIXER, GRADE TWO, and that struck Harry as being pretty ironic. The security guard handed Harry back his papers.

"I got my job to do, chum, and you got yours. All we can do is do our jobs the best we can. Am I right?"

He looked at Harry as if he expected an answer. Harry only shrugged.

"Well?" persisted the security guard. "Am I right?"

A number of the other bears had begun to whisper among themselves and to point at Harry. A small cub tugged at his mother's sleeve, saying, "Look, mommy, that fat bear has a sign with 'SPY' written on it pinned to his cloak!"

"Hush, dear," said the cub's mother. "You'll embarrass the poor thing!"

"Hush, dear. You'll embarrass the poor thing!"

"Well?" said the security guard, frowning down at Harry. "What about it?"

"You're right! You're right!" said Harry, waving his hands. "I'm sorry I brought it up!"

"Darn right I'm right," muttered the guard, and, much to Harry's relief, he went on his way.

Harry stared out of the window to see if he could locate the agent he was supposed to contact: Agent Ten

Zero Zero Three, otherwise known as Fred. Harry had worked with Fred many times before and liked him very much, except for his habit of overdoing spy precautions and making everything considerably more complicated than it really needed to be. Outside of this small, persistent flaw in Fred's professional technique, he possessed many excellent qualities, and Harry felt fortunate in having drawn him as an assistant. But search as he might, he was unable to see any sign of Fred outside.

Harry got his suitcase from the overhead rack and walked out of the car slowly, not sure just what to do. There was a short, odd-looking tree growing on the platform nearby. Harry walked over so that he might stand in its shade while he waited for Fred to turn up. But he found that the stubby, little branches cast no shade at all. Irritated, Harry decided to lean against the tree and get a little rest. Harry sighed and leaned back, but the tree almost fell over. Harry shook his head at the silly thing and went back to peering this way and that for a sign of Fred.

Suddenly, without warning, the tree began to make a strange, muffled noise. Harry looked at it closely. He

The tree was trying to speak!

was not sure, but it seemed to him that the tree was trying to speak! He tapped at it and moved it gently, this way and that. The muffled noise continued and, listening carefully, Harry realized it was coming from a knothole near the top of the tree. A small, leafy branch had fallen into the knothole and plugged it up almost completely. Harry tugged at the branch and it popped out of the knothole like a cork from a bottle. A puffing and gasping sound came from the knothole for a minute, and then, in a faint but steady voice, the tree said, "It certainly is hot for being around Christmastime."

Harry peered into the tree and saw two blue eyes looking out at him.

"Fred!"

"Never mind that, Harry," said Fred. For, sure enough, it was Fred in there. "What's the countersignal?"

Harry sighed. Fred was a perfectionist when it came to signals and countersignals and would never tolerate any shortcuts.

"Yes, but that's what happens when you make a goose wear a straw hat," said Harry, giving the countersignal. He knew there was no use trying to hurry Fred along.

*"Never mind that, Harry.
What's the countersignal?"*

"You're better than Pennsylvania, Bearmania," recited Fred in the tree.

> You're better than Transylvania, Bearmania.
> You're better than any of those places.

"It's good to see you, Fred," said Harry.

"It's good to see you too, Harry," said Fred. "Boy, I'm sure glad you came along when you did and pulled that branch out of my knothole. I almost smothered in here."

Harry shook his head sympathetically. A small crowd of curious bears had gathered to watch him talking to the tree.

"I don't think it's healthy for trees to grow on railroad station platforms," said one of the bears. "That's probably why it talks to people. It's not well."

three The Terrible Green Bear

Getting Fred off the station platform in his tree disguise was not as difficult as Harry thought it might be. After several unsuccessful attempts to lift him up and carry him—"I think that fat bear's trying to steal that silly-looking tree!" the crowd had begun whispering—Harry merely ambled slowly down the platform and let Fred hobble along after him as best he could, which was really not very well. Since no bear there, and probably no bear in the entire history of the world, had ever seen a walking tree, none of the crowd quite knew what to do about it. Most of them, after a startled glance or two, pretended they hadn't noticed anything peculiar at all.

There was one bear, however, who watched Fred steadily as he made his way to the station. This was a very thin, pale bear wearing a long red beard and a floppy checkered coat and carrying a large black trunk bound in brass. The trunk seemed to be very heavy as the bear carried it only with the greatest of difficulty.

One bear watched Fred steadily.

Every so often he would set the trunk down and pull out a huge handkerchief and wipe his forehead. But he never once let his eyes waver from the sight of Fred in his tree disguise.

Harry slowed down a little so that Fred could catch up and then whispered into Fred's knothole, "I think you're being watched, Fred."

Fred made a muffled snort and shook his branches rather impatiently.

"Of course, I'm being watched, Harry. Why do you think I'm wearing this fool thing? They have me under their gaze twenty-four hours a day."

Harry glanced nervously back at the pale bear, who had once again lifted his trunk and was staggering after them.

"Who has you under their gaze twenty-four hours a day, Fred?" asked Harry.

"The agents of the Terrible Green Bear, Harry!" was the whispered reply.

Harry swallowed and cleared his throat. Then he thoughtfully pulled out a macaroon and chewed it as he trudged along. He hadn't bargained on having anything to do with something called the Terrible Green Bear. It sounded awfully scary, and he wasn't really sure he was up to it. However, he reminded himself sternly, he was a spy, after all, and spies do have to deal with scary things now and then, even though they might rather not. He cleared his throat again, and in a voice he hoped was firm and confident-sounding, he asked, "How many agents does this Terrible Green Bear have, offhand?"

"Dozens," whispered Fred, "at least. Maybe even hundreds. And all of them carry trunks."

"Ah, yes," said Harry, sneaking a look back at the thin, pale bear behind them and at the trunk he was lugging along.

By this time they had reached the station, which adjoined the National Macaroon Factory. It was a busy place with many bears coming and going, most of them engaged in errands having to do with the manufacture and distribution of macaroons. A very pleasant, sugary smell pervaded the atmosphere, and Harry licked his lips and raised his nose straight up into the air so that he might take a nice big sniff of it.

"No time for that now, Harry," hissed Fred from inside his tree disguise. "Follow me. We'll give him the slip. We have an important appointment with the head of the Macaroon Factory in a matter of minutes!"

Harry licked his lips.

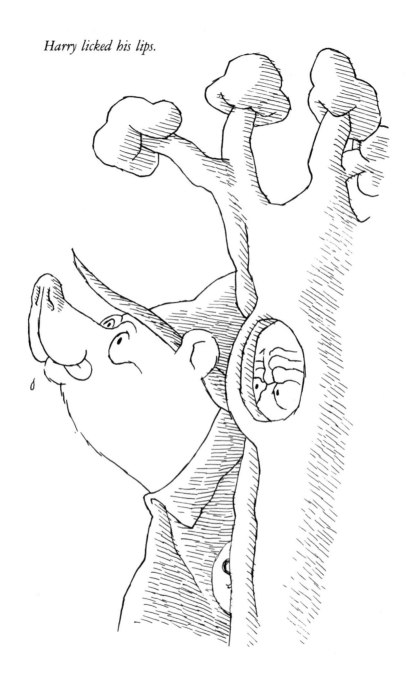

This time Fred took the lead and Harry followed after. It was amazing how well Fred had gotten the knack of getting around in his tree disguise. They crossed the main waiting room of the station and entered a small tunnel. The tunnel was rather dark and grew darker the further they entered it because the lights in the ceiling ahead were spaced farther and farther apart.

"Where does this tunnel lead, Fred?" asked Harry.

"It doesn't lead anywhere, Harry. That's why you'll notice there's nobody else taking it. It's a dead end."

"Then why are we walking down it if it doesn't lead anywhere, Fred?"

"Because for *us* it leads somewhere, Harry," he said, and Harry could see one of Fred's blue eyes wink through the knothole.

Fred walked up to the wall and pressed on one of its granite blocks and then on another.

"Watch this, Harry," he said, only nothing happened.

"I don't get it, Fred. What are you trying to do?"

"Wait a second," said Fred, his voice tightening a little, and he pushed at the wall as he had done before. Once again, nothing happened.

"What's—" began Harry, but Fred interrupted him rather testily.

"There's supposed to be a secret panel here, is what," he said. "Only it looks like there isn't!"

Anxiously, he began to push at various parts of the stone wall. "Why can't they ever tell you anything *right?*" he hissed.

"Don't you think—" Harry began, but he was interrupted once more, not by Fred, but by the floor opening up beneath his feet.

four The Mysterious Macaroon Change

Directly beneath the hole which had suddenly opened in the floor was a smooth, curving slide, and Harry found himself gliding quickly down its slope into a darkness which became more and more spooky as he went along.

"I wish," sighed Harry, the air whistling past his ears and making them wiggle, "that I had never become a spy. I wish I had listened to my mother. She knew what she was talking about when she told me I should become a tap dancer. Why didn't I listen to her?"

Suddenly, behind and above him, Harry heard a clattering and banging sound. At first he wondered what it was. Then he realized it must be poor Fred in his tree disguise.

"Poor Fred," said Harry to himself. "It's tough enough being in a spot like this without being dressed up like a tree."

Suddenly Harry saw a bright opening ahead, and the next thing he knew he had shot out through it into a surprisingly pleasant little room, full of well-stuffed, cozy-looking furniture. He had had only a chance for a quick look around when Fred's tree disguise landed on the floor beside him with a thump.

"Are you all right, Fred?" Harry asked, bending over the tree disguise, but the tree disguise just lay there, silent and ominously still. "Speak to me, Fred!" Harry cried, rapping on the tree disguise's bark and producing a hollow sound.

"I'm still in the tunnel, Harry!" Fred's voice came out from the opening in the wall. "I'm afraid to come out!"

"It's much nicer in here than it is in the tunnel," said Harry.

"Are you sure?"

"Yes, it's very nice. As a matter of fact, it's kind of cozy."

"All right then," said Fred. And he slipped out of the hole into the room and stood beside Harry.

*It was a surprisingly
pleasant little room.*

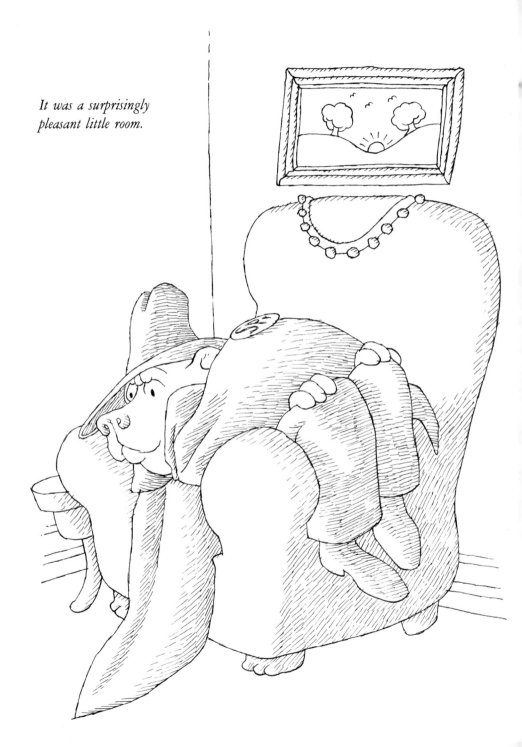

Fred was a fairly ordinary-looking bear except for the deep frown lines in his forehead which probably came from his always wanting everything to work out exactly right. Naturally, he wore a black slouch hat and a cloak like Harry, although his were considerably rumpled from having been worn inside of the tree disguise. He brushed at his clothes and looked around at the room.

"Say, you're right," he said. "It is nice in here."

"I'm so glad you like it," said a new voice, and Harry and Fred turned to see a dear, sweet old lady bear walk daintily into the room.

She wore an apron and had glasses perched on the end of her nose, and the snow white hair on the top of her head was done up in a bun. She carried a tray with a pot of tea and three cups on it, plus a big covered plate.

"I thought you boys could do with a little refreshment," she said, smiling.

"Oh, it's *you*, Mrs. Sweetly!" said Fred. "I thought it was going to turn out that the Terrible Green Bear had got us!"

Fred turned to Harry.

"Harry," he said, "this is Mrs. Sweetly. She is in charge of the macaroon production line and the only one in Bearmania who knows the secret formula for

"I thought you boys could do with a little refreshment."

making the macaroons which are our national pride and joy."

Harry looked at the dear old lady with affection and respect. "Very pleased to meet you, Mrs. Sweetly."

"And I'm pleased to meet you, Harry, I'm sure," she said. "Fred's told me so many nice things about you. I certainly hope that you and he can manage to do something about that awful Green Bear."

"It's 'Terrible,' Mrs. Sweetly," corrected Fred.

"Yes, it certainly is," she said, carefully arranging the tea things and the covered plate on a table. "Do you like macaroons, young bear?" she asked Harry.

"Yes, ma'm," said Harry. "As a matter of fact, they are my favorite food."

"Well, then," said Mrs. Sweetly, removing the cover from the big plate, "perhaps you will be able to eat some of these."

Harry reached out a paw and then drew back in astonishment. The macaroons on the plate were fine, plump, rich, obviously juicy macaroons, macaroons which were clearly as well-made and tasty as macaroons can possibly get to be. Yet Harry could not bring himself to pick up one and pop it into his mouth, for all the macaroons were colored an awful, absolutely terrible and positively disgusting shade of green!

Mrs. Sweetly looked at Harry's expression and sighed.

"They're all like that these days," she said. "Every-

*The macaroons were a
disgusting shade of green.*

one of them that comes off the line. And we don't have
a clue why!"

"We have the letters, Mrs. Sweetly," said Fred. He

reached under his cloak and produced a small bundle of papers which he handed to Harry. "Just look at these!"

There were three letters in all. The first one looked like this:

HELP!
I AM
TURNING GREEN!
SOMEBODY STOP IT!
SOMEBODY BETTER
STOP IT!
(SIGNED)
THE TURNING GREEN BEAR

"That was found nailed to the outer entrance of the National Macaroon Factory, if you can imagine such a thing!" sniffed Mrs. Sweetly.

The second letter read:

HELP! I AM
ENTIRELY GREEN! I AM
NOT GOING TO STAND FOR
THIS! I HAD BETTER NOT
BE GREEN TOMORROW OR
I WILL DO SOMETHING
TERRIBLE!
(SIGNED)
THE GREEN BEAR

"Where did you find this one?" asked Harry.

"On the inner entrance to the National Macaroon Factory!" said Fred.

The third letter went as follows:

ALRIGHT
FOR YOU!
I AM STILL GREEN
AND I HAVE DONE
SOMETHING
TERRIBLE
JUST LIKE I SAID!!!
(SIGNED)
THE TERRIBLE
GREEN BEAR

"This one was found on the main oven of the production line of the National Macaroon Factory, Harry," said Fred, and an ominous tone came into his voice. "And when the macaroons came out that morning, they were all colored a terrible *green!*"

five Harry Takes Notes

After tea Mrs. Sweetly took Harry and Fred on a tour of the National Macaroon Factory. Harry was very impressed. Everything was efficient and orderly. Yet at the same time there was a comfortable, homelike atmosphere about the place. The main sugar dispenser was a marvelous modern machine, for example, but it had a very pretty pattern painted on it and there were vases of flowers on the control board.

"We have gotten the production up to twenty-five macaroons a minute," said Mrs. Sweetly proudly. But then her face grew sad. "However, they are all colored that miserable shade of green and nobody will eat them."

Harry watched macaroons coming out of one of the side ovens one after another on a conveyor belt. Sure enough, there was not a one of them which was not green, although Harry noticed with interest that some of them seemed to be greener than others. Then, as he looked around, he saw a very large, rather lumpy-

Lovable Old Bill.

looking bear sweeping the floor with a broom, at the base of a huge egg beater.

"Who is that?" Harry asked.

"Why that's Lovable Old Bill," said Mrs. Sweetly, smiling again. "I don't know what we'd do here without Lovable Old Bill. He cleans up and fixes things and I don't know what all. He showed up after our last janitor, Boris, left and just took over Boris's job and more."

"Why did Boris leave?" asked Harry, taking out a notepad from under his cloak and writing *boris* on it.

"No reason at all that we could tell," said Mrs. Sweetly. "One day he was here, and the next he wasn't."

Harry wrote *no reason* in his notebook, then folded it shut and put it back under his cloak.

"I was quite upset about it," Mrs. Sweetly continued. "And I certainly was glad when Lovable Old Bill came by asking for a job."

Lovable Old Bill had been patiently sweeping along and was now quite close to them. Mrs. Sweetly called him over and introduced him to Harry and Fred. He looked even larger and lumpier close-up. He had a kindly smile which never seemed to change.

"I certainly hope you fellows manage to stop all these macaroons from turning green," said Lovable Old Bill.

After they had completed their tour of the factory, Mrs. Sweetly went back to her regular duties and Harry and Fred went for a little walk to talk things over.

"I believe there is a connection between those notes from the Terrible Green Bear and the macaroons turning green, Fred," said Harry.

"Yes, Harry," said Fred, "I certainly go along with you on that."

"What's more," continued Harry, "I believe he is making the macaroons green in order to revenge his being made green. Do you follow me?"

"Yes, I do, Harry," said Fred. "It all makes perfect sense."

They walked on a little while longer in silence. Then Harry said, "So the way to stop the macaroons from turning green is to catch the Terrible Green Bear."

"I think you've put it all in a nutshell, Harry," said Fred. Then his voice sank to a whisper. "We're being followed, Harry."

"We're being followed, Harry."

"What's that, Fred? I didn't hear what you said."

"We're being followed, Harry," Fred said a little louder.

Harry peeked back over his shoulder and, sure enough, there was somebody following them down the street. It was a bear with a huge moustache and thick glasses, wearing a formal evening suit complete with a tall silk hat and carrying a large black trunk bound in brass.

"He's carrying a trunk just like that bear at the station," said Harry.

"A sure sign he's one of the agents of the Terrible Green Bear, Harry."

Harry pulled out one of the few nongreen macaroons he had brought with him and chewed on it thoughtfully. Then he turned again to look at the bear following him, and the bear, apparently alarmed by this second inspection, disappeared quickly into an alleyway.

"I think I frightened him off," said Harry.

"There'll be another one, Harry," said Fred. "There always is."

Sure enough, out of the alleyway into which the bear wearing the evening suit had gone came a bear wearing

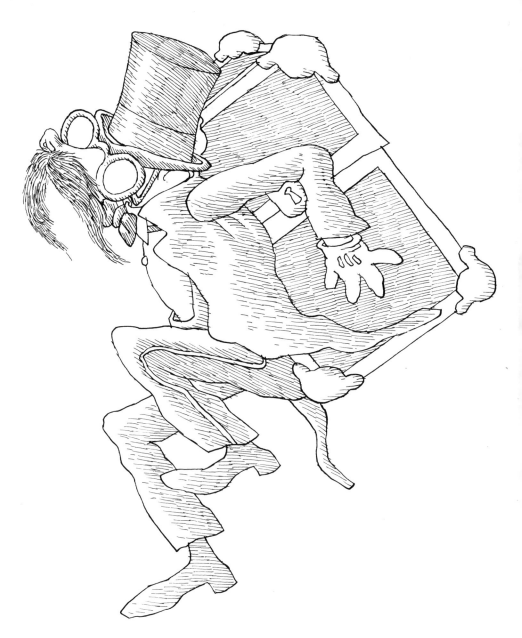

Sure enough, there was somebody following them.

a long orange burnoose and a fez and a curly white
beard. This bear was also carrying a large black trunk
bound in brass.

"You're certainly right about there being a lot of
those agents," said Harry.

"He must have a regular army of them, Harry," said
Fred. "Yet I've never seen more than one of them at a
time."

Harry took out his notepad and carefully wrote

lots of agents

Then he looked up at the sky, pursed his lips,
frowned, and added

with trunks.

after which he closed up the notebook and put it away.

six Captain Jack

One of the most important things about being a good spy, Harry believed, was to keep up-to-date. In order to do this, Harry spent a good deal of his spare time reading up on the latest gadgets science had produced and then seeing how they might be applied to his own trade.

Lately, in the papers Harry had noticed stories concerning the Bearmania Lighter than Air Force and its hero, Captain Jack. Captain Jack had been trying to perfect a device he called the Explorer Balloon. Unlike all previous balloons, which floated whichever way the wind happened to be blowing, this one would go just

In his spare time Harry read up on the latest gadgets.

where you wanted it to, or at least nearby, thanks to an ingenious arrangement of paddlewheels and vanes.

It had struck Harry that Captain Jack's invention would come in very handy for spying. But since the Bearmania Lighter than Air Force Headquarters was a long way from where Harry lived, he had done nothing about it. Now, however, he had traveled a long way from where he lived in order to get to the National

Macaroon Factory, and right next door to the factory
was nothing less than the Bearmania Lighter than Air
Force. It was too good a chance to miss.

When Harry and Fred returned from their little
walk, therefore—this time followed by a bear with long
blond hair wearing a shaggy fur coat and tennis shoes
and carrying a large black trunk bound in brass—they
did not go to the factory, but walked up to the building
next to it which had a small, slightly ragged piece of
paper taped to its front door with the following written
on it:

NOTICE   NOTICE
       BEARMANIA
   LIGHTER THAN AIR FORCE
     PLEASE RING BELL
IF NO ANSWER, INQUIRE AT
     DELICATESSEN
          THANK YOU

"I really expected something a little more impressive
than this," said Harry, looking dubiously at the building, which was a little run-down looking.

"Well, for a long time nobody believed you could fly," said Fred. "So maybe there are still a few holding out in the government. It's hard enough to get money for spying, and everybody believes in spying."

Harry rang the bell as the notice instructed and the two spies could hear a tiny tinkling sound in the depths of the building. There was a slight pause, and then came a terrific crashing followed by a series of thumps. Then there was a long pause.

"What do you suppose that was, Harry?" asked Fred.

"I can't imagine, Fred," said Harry.

Eventually the silence inside was broken by the sound of approaching footsteps and a door was opened to reveal an elderly, slightly chubby bear dressed in the uniform of a captain in the Bearmania Lighter than Air Force. The bear was obviously none other than Captain Jack himself.

"Excuse me for taking so long to answer the door, gentlemen," he said. "But the sound of the bell startled me—I have so few callers—and I am afraid the prototype winged surrey I was working on overbalanced and fell. I hope the noise didn't startle you."

Harry introduced himself and Fred to Captain Jack

It was Captain Jack himself.

and as the three bears entered the building, he explained their mission.

"Well, I certainly hope you manage to catch the Terrible Green Bear, if he is the one who is turning the macaroons green. I just can't eat them when they are that color, and I love macaroons. I've tried eating them with my eyes closed and thinking of something else. I've tried eating them in the dark. I've tried eating them with bread wrapped around them. But nothing seems to work."

Harry could only marvel at the ingenuity of the great inventor standing before him.

"I believe you may be able to help us in tracking down the Green Bear, sir," he said, and he told Captain Jack how he had read of him and his Explorer Balloon and how it had occurred to him that such a device might be useful in spying.

"I will be delighted to assist you," said Captain Jack. "Follow me, gentlemen, and I will lead you to the Explorer Balloon hangar."

They passed many interesting sights on their way to the hangar, including the winged surrey they had heard crash earlier. It lay on its side in a large room with one

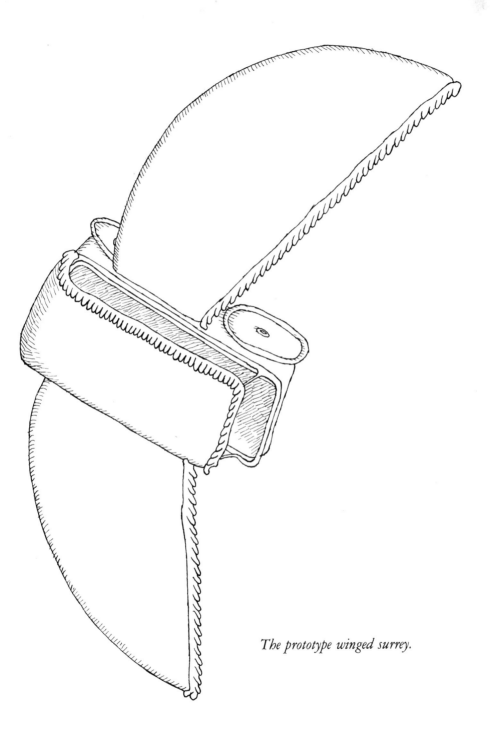

The prototype winged surrey.

wing stretched straight up and the other lying spread out on the floor.

"You'll notice I've put braided gold fringe on the wings to match the surrey top," said Captain Jack, "but I'm starting to think that the fringe slows it down and will have to go."

Among other fascinating sights, Harry and Fred saw a bird suit, a flying chair, and a beret with a propeller set into its top. Unfortunately, Captain Jack explained, none of these machines worked.

Then they entered a large barn attached to the rear of the building. Harry gasped! Before him was nothing less than the famous Explorer Balloon itself!

"Why it's beautiful!" he exclaimed.

"Thank you," said Captain Jack, and you could tell that he was pleased.

The balloon part of the machine looked like a big, upside-down pear, and it was painted gold with

painted on it in blue, which of course were the initials for Bearmania Lighter than Air Force. Suspended from the balloon was the cabin, which was also painted gold, and projecting from the sides and rear of the cabin were the paddlewheels and vanes with which the pilot could control the Explorer Balloon, and these were painted blue.

"Unlike so many of my other airships," said Captain Jack, "this one does fly."

"Just wait'll the Terrible Green Bear finds out he's going to have to deal with that," said Fred. "I'll bet he'll be plenty scared!"

seven An Unexpected Visitor

At that very moment, unknown to Harry or Fred or Captain Jack, a mysterious figure was clinging like a bug to the roof of the Explorer Balloon hangar, peering down at them through the skylight. The figure was wearing a sarape and a big Mexican hat, and beside it on the roof was a large black trunk bound in brass.

"Darn it!" snarled the mysterious figure. "Darn it! Darn it! *Darn it!*"

Then the mysterious figure, which of course was a bear, got control of itself and, pressing its ear to a pane of the skylight, listened intently to the three bears below. It was impossible to understand every word being spoken, but enough had been heard to clearly show that Captain Jack and his Explorer Balloon had joined the hunt for the Terrible Green Bear. This did not make the bear in the sarape and the Mexican hat at all happy.

The bear watched until the three below had left the hangar, and then, very carefully, and with considerable difficulty on account of the large black trunk, he worked his way to the ground. Once there, he stood by a window and looked thoughtfully in at the Explorer Balloon.

"What am I going to do?" he whispered to himself. "What am I going to *do?*"

He pondered the question, gritting his teeth and rubbing his hands, and then he snapped his fingers and gave a nasty chuckle.

"I've *got* it!" he hissed. "I'll sabotage the Balloon, and when Captain Jack goes up in it, he'll fall down pretty soon and bust the thing into a *million pieces!*"

This struck the bear as being very funny, and he had to hold both his paws over his face to stifle his giggles.

He snapped his fingers.

Meanwhile, Harry and Fred and Captain Jack were in the Captain's office, studying a map of the National Macaroon Factory and its surroundings. They had decided that Harry would keep the outside of the factory under observation while Fred would patrol its interior and Captain Jack would fly back and forth over the building and carefully watch all that was going on in the general area. If the Green Bear showed up, they reasoned, one or another of them was bound to spot him!

Once they had it all straight, they headed right back for the hangar to put their plan into action. They were halfway down the hall leading to the hangar when Harry stopped suddenly and his ears went up.

"What is it, Harry?" asked Fred.

"I thought I heard something," said Harry. "Is there anyone else in the building, Captain Jack?"

"No, there isn't, Harry. Unfortunately I am, at present, the only member of the Bearmania Lighter than Air Force and the only tenant here."

"There it is again!" said Harry, and this time the other bears heard it. It was an odd rustling noise, and it came from a doorway to their left.

"We were in there before," said Harry, "seeing some of your inventions."

"We know you're in there."

Then they all heard a muffled sneeze.

The three bears crowded by the doorway and looked into the darkened room. Harry cleared his throat and said, "All right, there, we know you're in there. Come out before I count to three or I'll—"

But Harry never got a chance to say what he would do when he got to three because, with a loud, flapping noise and a cloud of dust, out of the room burst what seemed to be a gigantic bird!

Harry and Fred were so astounded that they could only stand and gape, but Captain Jack shouted, "That's some bear wearing my bird suit! Stop him! It took me months to build that bird suit!" And that sent all three of them dashing down the hall after the weird-looking figure.

The bear in the bird suit ran well ahead, flapping his arms and sending out more clouds of dust. It was obvious that the suit needed a good cleaning. The bear in the bird suit sneezed uncontrollably, but that didn't seem to slow him up. He flapped down the hall and into the hangar, and then round and round it several times. And then the bird suit's wings began to flap faster and faster and the next thing that happened—to the astonishment of everybody including the bear in the

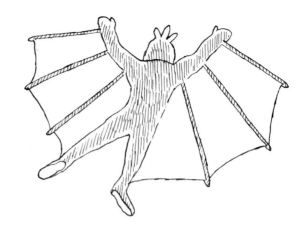

"He's flying!" cried Captain Jack.

bird suit—the bear in the bird suit began to rise up from the floor!

Captain Jack stopped in his tracks and looked up at the steadily rising figure.

"He's flying!" cried Captain Jack happily. "Oh, will you look at that! He's flying!"

"I thought that thing didn't work," shouted Harry, trying to grab at the feet of the bear in the bird suit but missing them by several inches.

"So did I," said Captain Jack. "But it *does* work. Oh, isn't it wonderful?"

"Yes," said Harry, looking unhappily up at the bear in the bird suit, who had now flown all the way up to the skylight and was working at its latch, "but he's getting away."

The bear in the bird suit pushed open the skylight and, with several powerful beats of the bird suit's wings, flew off into the blue.

"You're right, Harry," said Captain Jack. "Open the hangar doors. We'll catch him in the Explorer Balloon!"

eight Danger Aloft

Considering it was the first time Harry and Fred had tried to move the Explorer Balloon, they did a pretty good job of it. At one point they got it snagged in a tangle of ropes by the door, and at another they found themselves pushing it in opposite directions; but they did manage to get it out of the hangar with the flying bear in the bird suit still in sight, and that was what mattered.

"Climb in the ship, lads," cried Captain Jack, "while I loosen the hawsers!"

Harry and Fred clambered into the cabin of the Ex-

plorer Balloon while the air officer undid the ropes
which held the craft down in case of a sudden unexpected gust of wind. He had no sooner released the last
of them when a sudden unexpected gust of wind came
up and Harry and Fred found themselves abruptly lifted
into the air. Harry leaned out of the window and
shouted down to Captain Jack, "What should we do?"

"Go on without me, boys," Captain Jack called up to
them. "You'll never catch that bear if you have to come
back down for me. The pedals make the paddlewheels
go, and you steer her with the tiller."

"I'm not sure if I can manage it, Captain Jack!"
shouted Harry.

Captain Jack shouted something else, but by now
they were too far up to make out what it was. Harry
hoped it wasn't anything really important. He settled
himself at the controls and cleared his throat nervously.

"Are you sure you can pull this off, Harry?" asked
Fred.

"No, Fred, I'm not," said Harry.

The ship began to tilt ominously to one side. Harry
began to peddle and the paddlewheels outside moved
and the aircraft, much to Harry's relief, smoothly
righted itself.

"Are you sure you can pull this off, Harry?"

"Where's that bear in the bird suit got to, Fred?" asked Harry. "I've lost track of him in all this confusion."

"Over there to the left, Harry."

Sure enough, high in the sky and a little above them was the fleeing bear. Harry nervously moved the tiller and the Explorer Balloon's prow turned toward the small, flying figure.

"He seems to be heading for that swamp north of the city, Harry," said Fred.

"I wonder if that's where he wants to go," said Harry, "or if it's just where the bird suit's taking him."

The next actions of the bear in the bird suit seemed to clear that up as he began to do a peculiar, uneven kind of looping, which he probably would never have done if he could have avoided it. The loops consisted of sudden, sickening drops followed by a frantic flapping of wings to regain altitude.

"That looks awfully tiring," said Fred.

Harry continued to peddle and steer, and the Explorer Balloon steadily decreased the distance between them. The nearer they got, the clearer it was that the bear in the bird suit was unhappy. His legs, for instance, were pumping steadily, as if he were attempting to get a foothold in the air.

"I'm afraid he is in trouble," said Harry.

"Yes," said Fred, "but he does seem to be holding to a consistent direction."

Harry peered past the awkwardly flying bear.

"I believe you're right, Fred. I believe he's heading for that cabin out there in the swamp."

Far ahead of them was a disreputable-looking shack by the side of a dirt road, and it looked as if Harry was absolutely right about its being the bear in the bird suit's goal because every flap of his wings brought him closer to it.

When the flying bear got over the cabin, he began to descend in tiny stages, understandably trying to avoid landing in one drop. Then the front door of the cabin opened, and out came a figure which caused both Harry and Fred to gasp in surprise.

"It's him!" cried Fred. "Will you look at that!"

There in the clearing before the cabin, waving his arms furiously at the figure in the bird suit, was a bright green bear!

"Somehow, I never thought he'd actually be green," said Harry. "I thought he was using a kind of poetic license, trying to create an image."

"He's green, all right," said Fred. "And you can tell he doesn't want that flying bear to land by his cabin. Look at him trying to wave him away."

"Maybe he believes it's a giant bird attacking him," said Harry.

It was a green bear!

"No," said Fred. "You can see the bear has removed his bird helmet. It's obviously just a bear in a bird suit."

"Now the green bear's throwing rocks at him," said Harry. "That flying bear has led us straight to him and he's furious."

"Well, I guess this wraps up—" began Fred. But a loud, snapping noise made him stop and turn rather pale. "What's that, Harry?" he asked in a small voice.

The Explorer Balloon had begun to wobble in a peculiar way. Harry peered out the windows. There was another loud, snapping noise and the ship lurched to one side.

"I'm not enjoying this, Harry," said Fred.

"Someone has half sawed through the paddlewheel supports, Fred," said Harry. "And they are starting to break."

"I think I know who did that, Harry," said Fred.

"I believe I do too, Fred," said Harry.

The pedals which moved the paddlewheels were now hopelessly jammed, and the ship rolled slowly this way and that as the wind blew it where it would.

nine Scary Surprises

"Well, that's just dandy," said Harry disgustedly, looking at the cabin of the Terrible Green Bear going further and further into the distance, "that's really just swell."

"How are we going to get down, Harry?" asked Fred.

"I don't know, Fred," Harry answered, studying the control panel. "There are quite a few knobs and levers here, but they don't have any labels on them."

"I suppose it wouldn't be a good idea to guess, considering our situation," said Fred.

"I think it would be ill-advised," said Harry.

They drifted on for several minutes in silence. Then Fred said, "Harry, I just had a thought."

"What's that, Fred?"

"Well, considering that bear sawed through the paddlewheel supports, isn't it possible he's done something else to the ship?"

Harry rubbed his chin thoughtfully. He had run out

of nongreen macaroons and wished he hadn't. He felt he could really use a macaroon right now. "That's a very disturbing thought, Fred," he said.

The two spies began to look carefully about them. First they examined the flooring; then they looked at the walls and windows and ceiling; then they peered out of the windows at the cables holding the balloon to the cabin.

"I think I see what he's been up to, Harry," said Fred.

"I believe I do too, Fred," said Harry.

Several of the cables were very badly frayed, as if they had been rubbed with a file or something else very rough. One or two of them looked as though they were just about to give. Harry opened the window next to the worst-looking cable and peered at it closely.

"I wouldn't touch it, Harry," said Fred. "That might be all it needs."

"Still we have to do something," said Harry, and as if to underline the statement, the cable parted with a tiny snap.

"Oh dear," said Fred.

"I think," said Harry, "this changes things about taking chances with the controls."

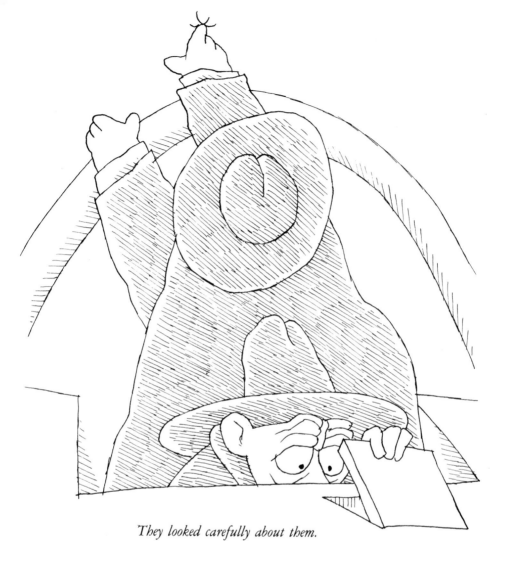

They looked carefully about them.

He gave the control panel a long hard look.

"Which of these things looks to you as if it would make the ship descend, Fred?" he asked.

"Perhaps that lever, there," said Fred.

Harry reached out and touched the lever and there was a sudden, earsplitting blast of noise which startled both the bears rather badly.

"Maybe we'd best leave off fooling with these controls," said Fred and then winced as another cable parted.

"I'm afraid we can't afford to do that, Fred," said Harry. "Perhaps this knob here will do the trick."

Harry turned the knob a little, but nothing seemed to happen. He moved it a little more and then the bears became aware of a faint hissing noise.

"What do you suppose that is, Harry?" asked Fred.

"I don't know, Fred," said Harry, clearing his throat. "It seems to be coming from above."

He leaned out the window and looked up.

"I think the balloon is leaking, Fred."

"Oh?" said Fred, but he could hardly be heard.

Another cable snapped.

"Er, maybe if I turn the knob back the balloon will stop leaking," said Harry.

"I guess it really doesn't matter much if the balloon leaks or not, Harry," said Fred, in a tiny choked voice, "because it looks as if we're going to be separated from it at any minute."

Another cable snapped.

"I'm afraid you're right, Fred," said Harry, watching another cable, and then another after that one, snap. They were now hanging from the balloon by one, badly frayed, cable. "I'm sorry things worked out like this, Fred," said Harry.

"All part of the business, Harry," said Fred. And

then the last cable parted and the cabin of the Explorer Balloon started to fall.

Suddenly there was a snap and a banging from the cabin roof, and Harry looked out and up to see that the force of the air rushing by had pulled a panel off the roof and that from the opening out rushed a huge quantity of bright orange silk.

"Something or other's happening, Fred," said Harry.

The silk puffed out and spread over the cabin like a huge umbrella, held to the cabin by more than a dozen sturdy-looking ropes, and the cabin immediately stopped its fast downward plunge and began a leisurely descent.

"For heaven's sake," cried Harry. "It's an automatic parachute!"

"Well, I'm certainly glad to hear *that*, Harry," said Fred.

ten Plans Pay Off

The next morning at the National Macaroon Factory, Harry and Fred brought Mrs. Sweetly up-to-date on their adventures so far.

"So we landed in a farmer's field," said Harry. "And the balloon, which I'd opened the vents on by turning that knob, came down shortly after and settled right next to the cabin, just as neat as you please."

"So we put the whole thing on the farmer's cart and took it back to town with no harm done at all," said Fred. "Except for what that bear did to it, of course."

"And Captain Jack put that right," said Harry. "And he's up there doing his air patrol at this very moment."

"Well, that's just wonderful," said Mrs. Sweetly, "but what about that cabin in the swamp? Did you go back for another look?"

"All we found were the bird suit and some green splotches."

"Indeed we did, Mrs. Sweetly," said Harry. "But they'd cleared out. All we found were the bird suit and some green splotches on the floor and walls. I guess that's the stuff he colors the macaroons with."

"I'll bet that bear had had enough of that bird suit," said Fred.

At this point Lovable Old Bill came up with his broom and his kindly smile.

"Did you send for me, Mrs. Sweetly?" he asked.

"Yes, I did, Lovable Old Bill," she replied. "Harry and Fred here are going to do some spying today and find out if they can track down the Terrible Green Bear, and I want you to give them all the help you can."

"I'll be glad to lend a paw," said the lumpy bear. "Just say the word and I'll pitch right in."

"Thank you, Lovable Old Bill," said Harry. "I'd appreciate it if you'd tag along with Fred the first few times he patrols the factory and point out any areas he might miss."

"You bet," said Lovable Old Bill. "I'll put him wise."

Satisfied that Fred's end of things was well taken care of, Harry left the building and began his first walk around it. He'd gotten about halfway when he looked up and saw Captain Jack fly across the street above him. He waved at the Explorer Balloon, but the machine went out of sight over the roof of another building, missing its edge by inches. Captain Jack hadn't seemed to notice him.

"I guess he's got plenty to look at from up there," thought Harry to himself. "Easy enough to miss one waving bear."

Harry pulled out his notebook and consulted it as he went along. He had written down a few things last night which he figured would be important to bear in mind. He had, for example, put down

green spots

and that meant that he should keep his eyes open for anything looking like the stains and splotches he had come across in the swamp cabin. Then again, he had written

trunk-carrying bears

which of course referred to that odd habit the agents of the Terrible Green Bear had of carrying large black trunks bound in brass. He looked up from this last note and saw, to his astonishment, nothing less than a bear carrying a large black trunk bound in brass!

The bear was dressed up as a South American gaucho, with furry chaps and spurs and a long moustache curled at the ends. He had spotted Harry and was scuttling around the corner as fast as he could go. Harry took after him at once, but when he rounded the corner he could see no sign of him. Then he looked up and saw a bear dressed in denim coveralls rubbing furiously at a window with a floppy red cloth. There was a large black trunk bound in brass resting on the windowsill beside him.

"I see you," shouted Harry, pointing up at the bear on the windowsill. "You can't fool me!"

"What's that?" said the bear on the windowsill. "I'm afraid I didn't catch what you said, there."

"You heard what I said, all right," shouted Harry. "And I know you're an agent of the Terrible Green Bear too!"

"I'm sorry, buddy," said the bear on the windowsill,

There was a terrible bumping noise.

"I just can't make out a single word you're saying!"
And suddenly he shot open the window and zipped inside.

"You come back here!" shouted Harry, trying to
climb the wall. Above him there was a terrible bumping noise as the bear tried to pull his trunk through the
open window.

"Darn it! Darn it! *Darn it!*" he cried. And then he
missed his grip on the trunk and then grabbed it again.
And then down came both the trunk and the bear on
the sidewalk with a crash.

eleven Mean Edwin

The capture of the bear with the trunk proved a significant breakthrough in many ways. First, an examination of the contents of the trunk produced a startling revelation, for in it, among many other costumes, were:

A floppy checkered coat and a long red beard

A formal evening suit with a tall silk hat and a huge moustache and thick glasses

A long orange burnoose and a fez and a curly white beard

A sarape and a big Mexican hat

A South American gaucho suit with furry chaps and spurs and a long moustache curled up at the ends.

"I think," said Harry to Fred and Captain Jack, after carefully examining these varied disguises, "that we must seriously revise our thinking concerning the number of agents in the employ of the Terrible Green Bear."

"I guess you've come to pretty much the same conclusion I have, eh, Harry?" said Fred.

"I believe so, Fred. I think we'll have to revise our estimate of the number of agents downward considerably. Instead of there being hundreds of agents, or dozens, or even a couple, I have come to the conclusion that there is probably only one."

"I'll have to admit that comes as something of a relief, Harry," said Fred.

"Yes," said Harry. "It does simplify the case considerably."

"You're wrong there, you dumb bears!" cried the agent, who sat before them, carefully tied in a chair in Mrs. Sweetly's office at the National Macaroon Factory. "There's millions of us. You wait and see!"

"The fellow's obviously lying," said Captain Jack, moving in close on the bear in the chair. "See how his eyes are shifting back and forth?"

"See how his eyes are shifting back and forth?"

"You're right, Captain Jack," said Harry. "They do shift."

At that moment the door opened and Mrs. Sweetly came in.

"I heard you caught—" she began, and then she saw the bear tied in the chair and frowned and put her paws on her hips. "Well, I don't wonder!" she said.

"Do you know this bear, Mrs. Sweetly?" asked Harry.

"I do, I'm sorry to say," said the dear old lady bear. "And I am not surprised to learn that he sank to becoming an agent of the Terrible Green Bear. His name is Mean Edwin, and he certainly lives up to it."

"How's that, Mrs. Sweetly?" asked Harry.

"If there is a mean way to do anything, from saying hello, to making coffee, to putting on his hat, Mean Edwin will find a way to do it," said Mrs. Sweetly. "He worked here in the factory for two weeks last year, and it was at least that many months before we managed to get things back to normal. He put sugar in the salt bin and salt in the sugar bin. He mixed egg yolks in the egg whites so they wouldn't beat up fluffy. He even put walnuts in with the almonds. And that's just a start of the naughty things he did while he worked for us."

Everybody looked at Mean Edwin in disapproval, but Mean Edwin only sneered at them and said, "You just wait, you dummies! The Terrible Green Bear's going to get you good! Turning macaroons green is just the start, see? He's going to turn *everything* green, he is! Everything in the *world!*"

Mrs. Sweetly shook her head sadly and sighed.

He even put walnuts in with the almonds.

"Poor Mean Edwin," she said. "And poor us, for having to put up with poor Mean Edwin."

"There may be hope, Mrs. Sweetly," said Harry. "They have produced some wonderful cures in the National Hospital for Mean Bears. We shall have him sent there and see what happens."

Naturally the idea of being turned into a nice bear made Mean Edwin even more furious, but there wasn't much he could do about it but snarl, which he did. "Snarf!"

Fred went back to patrolling the interior of the factory, and Mrs. Sweetly went back to her regular tasks; but Harry and Captain Jack held a conference and it was decided that it would be a good idea if Harry went up with the aviator so that he might apply his special spy training to the bird's eye view from the balloon. Harry questioned Captain Jack on what he had seen so far as they readied the ship.

"Nothing much unexpected," said Captain Jack. "However, I was surprised to observe an extensive roof garden on top of the National Macaroon Factory."

"Strange," said Harry. "I'd have thought Mrs. Sweetly would have mentioned something like that. Perhaps they use it for growing almonds."

Captain Jack settled himself at the controls and worked the elevation control—it turned out to be a lever in the middle of the panel—and they began to rise.

"Any place in particular you would like to go?" asked Captain Jack.

"Just take more or less the same route you did this morning, Captain Jack," said Harry, "and if I get any ideas I will let you know."

The ship started up at a sharp angle and then suddenly shifted to the left to miss a lamp pole.

"That's coming awfully close," thought Harry to himself. "But then I suppose that's how a daring pilot such as Captain Jack flies."

A few moments later they grazed the tip of a large church steeple. Harry stifled a frightened squeak.

"It's silly of me to be nervous," Harry thought to himself. "After all, Captain Jack is an expert flyer. Everybody knows that."

But one minute later, when the Explorer Balloon barely missed running smack into the huge sign on the roof of the National Macaroon Factory, Harry was unable to entirely muffle a yelp.

"What's wrong, Harry?" asked Captain Jack.

"That's coming awfully close," thought Harry.

"Oh, excuse me, Captain Jack," said Harry, smiling and wiping his brow as unobtrusively as he could. "I suppose I'm a little keyed up and all, but I could have sworn we were going to run right into that sign!"

Captain Jack peered at Harry in puzzlement.

"What sign, Harry?" he asked.

twelve Important Discoveries

"Er, Captain Jack," said Harry, "would you mind slowing the ship as much as possible?"

"Not at all, Harry," said the Captain, decreasing the forward speed so that the Explorer Balloon almost hung suspended in the air.

"Thank you, Captain Jack. And now, could you tell me what that is over there, please?" asked Harry, pointing at the face of the enormous clock which was set into the center tower of the National Macaroon Factory, which was only three yards from where the Explorer Balloon hovered.

Captain Jack squinted in the direction Harry pointed.

"Some sort of a building, isn't it?" he asked at last.

"Can you make out anything white and round, Captain?" asked Harry.

"Yes, now that you mention it," said Captain Jack, smiling, "I do believe I can."

Harry nodded to himself. It was obvious Captain Jack needed a pair of spectacles in the worst way, and once they got down to the ground, he was resolved that Captain Jack would get them. But now there was something else to do, for Harry remembered something Captain Jack had said.

"Would you mind showing me the roof garden you saw on top of the National Macaroon Factory, Captain Jack?" asked Harry. "Only I'd appreciate it if you'd fly slowly as I'm a little keyed up, as I said."

"Certainly, Harry." Captain Jack touched a control and very slowly they rose over the edge of the roof, almost touching it, and then higher so that the roof lay spread out beneath them.

"There's the garden." Captain Jack pointed. "Over there."

Harry felt a thrill go through him, for there was no garden there, but a large area covered with blotchy green stains just like those he and Fred had found in the swamp cabin. It was also the same color that the

macaroons had lately turned to. He was looking at the very place where the Terrible Green Bear did his nasty work!

"Are those almond trees, Harry?" asked Captain Jack, squinting down at the green blotches. "They don't quite look like almond trees to me."

Later, when they had landed, Harry asked Mrs. Sweetly if she had a spare pair of glasses, and she did and she loaned them to Captain Jack at Harry's request. They looked tiny and odd on Captain Jack's rather large nose, but they worked. Captain Jack's eyes sparkled and he looked happily about him.

"Why, these are marvelous things!" he said. "Why, I had no idea everything had so many details! Thank you very much, Harry, for pointing these out to me. I shall certainly get a pair for myself!"

Then Harry and Fred and Captain Jack went up to the roof to look at the green stains. On the way they met Lovable Old Bill coming down the staircase. The lumpy bear seemed a little startled to see them, but the kindly smile on his face never changed.

"Well, gosh, I am sure glad to run into you fellows," he said. "Say, can I give you guys a hand?"

"No, that's all right, Lovable Old Bill," said Harry. "We are just on our way up to look around the roof."

"Heck, you know something? I forgot to show your pal Fred here the roof the other day! Boy," said Lovable Old Bill, "what a dumb bunny I am!" And he hurried down the stairs into the factory.

When Harry, Fred, and Captain Jack reached the top step, they paused for a moment. Then taking a deep breath, Harry flung open the door to the roof.

"Good grief," said Captain Jack. "This is no almond tree grove! What a ninny you must have thought me!"

"Not at all, Captain Jack," said Harry. "That you could fly the Explorer Balloon that well and needing glasses as badly as you did proves that you are a great pilot."

"Why, thank you, Harry," said Captain Jack.

"Harry," said Fred, "come over here. I think I may have found something."

Fred was holding a piece of hose which led from the water tower to a hole in the roof, and, around the hole in the roof, the green splotches were at their thickest. Harry looked up at the water tank, and then at the hole. Then he got down on his paws and knees and peered through the hole.

"I think I may
have found something."

"Can you guess what's down there," asked Harry, "directly beneath this hole?"

"I think I can, Harry," said Fred. "The main mixing vat. Am I right?"

Harry stood up trying to brush the green stains off his knees.

"Nothing else, Fred," said Harry. "And, unless I miss my guess, and I don't think I do, that water tank isn't full of water at all, but full of Terrible Green Bear green dye!"

The three bears looked up at the tank. And for the first time Harry noticed a rope stretched tight from the top of the water tank to a hook on the roof door.

"I imagine that's how he controls the flow of green dye from the tank," observed Harry.

"Dat iss right, chentlemen!" came a harsh, scratchy voice from behind the door. "Now I let *you* know how it feelink to be grin!"

And a green paw snaked out from the darkness in back of the door and pulled hard at the rope leading to the top of the tank filled with Terrible Green Bear dye!

thirteen Bad Luck for the Green Bear

The next few moments were green confusion and Harry never was able to sort the various events out in their proper order. But he would never forget looking up at the top of the tank and seeing it yawn slowly open to release a huge wave of the greenest green dye which had probably ever existed in the whole history of the world. The huge wave seemed to hang suspended in the air over Harry and Fred and Captain Jack for a moment, and then it hurtled down on them with a rush and splashing that swept them off their feet and sent them swirling in all directions.

"Watch out you don't get washed over the edge of the roof!" shouted Harry, but his voice was entirely drowned out by the roar of the gushing green dye. Around and around he went, looking at the sky above him and watching it spin through a haze of green foam.

Then, by degrees, the violence of the green dye's onrush decreased until there was only a gentle trickle of it

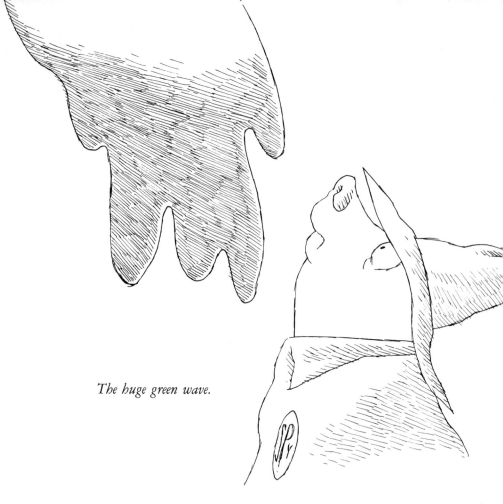

The huge green wave.

coming from the tank, and the three bears found themselves lying, shaken but unhurt, on various parts of the
roof.

Harry pushed himself up to a sitting position, took a
deep breath, blinked, let his breath out with a *whew,*
and looked around.

Except for the sky above, which was its good old re-
liable blue, absolutely *everything* that Harry could see,

was green. The asphalt on top of the roof was green. The little wall that ran around the edge of the roof was green. The door that led to the roof was green. The tank was green. Fred and Captain Jack were green and, he looked down at himself, so was Harry green.

He stood up and squeezed out his green cape, but it didn't help. He took off his green hat and green dye ran out over his green face. But it didn't make his face any greener because his face was already as green as it is possible for any face to get.

Harry walked over to where Fred was sitting.

"Are you all right, Fred?" he asked.

"Yes, except for being wet and green all over," said Fred. "I think I'll dry out pretty soon, but I don't know about getting over the green part."

Captain Jack seemed to be all right, except that the green dye had colored his glasses green and so everything he saw through them seemed to be green as well.

"Actually, it's not so bad," he said, looking up at the sky. "The clouds look something like emeralds and the sky is a little like the sea." The three bears made themselves as presentable as they could, seeing as how they were green, and then went down into the factory below.

As they made their entrance, all work stopped at once and everyone started to talk excitedly. Mrs. Sweetly came bustling up to them, full of concern.

"Oh, you poor dear bears!" she cried. "What on earth has happened to you?"

"It was only the last, desperate attempt on the part of the Terrible Green Bear to stop us from uncovering his identity, Mrs. Sweetly," said Harry, dripping a small pool of green dye where he stood.

"You mean you know who the Terrible Green Bear is?" cried Mrs. Sweetly, holding her hands together. "But who could it be?"

"The one person in the history of the National Macaroon Factory, as told by you, who cannot be accounted for, Mrs. Sweetly," said Harry. "The one who vanished without a trace, and for completely mysterious reasons."

"You mean—" said Mrs. Sweetly.

"Yes, Mrs. Sweetly," said Harry, "I mean Boris, the janitor who left you without explanation and was never seen again!"

"Boris Zptkxlikki!" said Mrs. Sweetly. "Why, who would have thought it?"

"Zptkxlikki, eh?" said Captain Jack. "I suppose that accounts for his accent."

Lovable Old Bill came up and shook Harry by the paw.

"I just knew you fellows would track down that Terrible Green Bear," he said enthusiastically. "Congratulations on a real great job well done, guys!"

Harry kept hold of Lovable Old Bill's large paw.

"But where has he been hiding, Harry?" asked Mrs. Sweetly. "And how has he managed to circulate among us without anybody knowing he's about?"

Lovable Old Bill began tugging a little to free his paw from Harry's, but Harry continued to hold on.

"He has been in plain sight all along, Mrs. Sweetly," said Harry. "In fact he's been one of the biggest sights around here. Think back, Mrs. Sweetly, what happened directly after the mysterious disappearance of Boris Zptkxlikki?"

"Why, I don't know," said the confused dear old lady bear.

"Would you please mind letting go of my paw, old buddy?" asked Lovable Old Bill, tugging a little harder to get loose.

"The equally mysterious appearance of Lovable Old Bill here, Mrs. Sweetly," said Harry.

"You mean—" said Mrs. Sweetly.

"Yes," said Harry, "I mean—"

At this dramatic moment, Lovable Old Bill gave a great, final tug, and staggered back free from Harry's grasp, leaving behind what seemed to be a large bear paw in Harry's paw. Lovable Old Bill looked down at the end of his arm, as did every bear there, and saw sticking out, for all to see, a bright green paw!

"Land sake!" cried Mrs. Sweetly. "Lovable Old Bill has been the Terrible Green Bear all along."

Lovable Old Bill staggered back.

fourteen Harry Is Happy

Boris Zptkxlikki, alias Lovable Old Bill, alias the Terrible Green Bear, tore off his Lovable Old Bill head mask with its fixed, kindly smile, to reveal his bright green head.

"All right, you gat me!" he snarled. "But dun't tink I am effen a liddle sorry for vat I done!"

"You know," said Captain Jack, taking off his green-tinted glasses, "there's something very familiar about the way that bear looks."

"He's green like you and me and Harry," said Fred impatiently.

"No, no, Fred, his green is a different green," said Harry.

"You turnink grin! Ha! How *you* like it!" cried Boris. "You don't like it *wan liddle bit! Nossir!*"

"What do you mean, Captain?" Harry asked Captain Jack. "What does he remind you of?"

"It's his color," said Captain Jack. "I've seen that exact shade of green before somewhere in my travels, but I can't remember just where."

"All right, you gat me!"

"If I am beink grin," continued Boris, annoyed by the attention Captain Jack and Harry were getting from the crowd, "why shouldn't macaroons beink grin? I ask myself this question. My answer? My answer is *there is absolutely no reason in world why macaroons shouldn't beink grin!*"

Harry signaled to Fred and he joined him and Captain Jack.

"It might have been on that exploring trip to Transylvania," Captain Jack scratched his head. "But no . . . ."

"SO I DID IT, SEE!" Boris was shouting now. "Every day, just after macaroon batter is beink finished, I go up on roof and dump in Terrible Grin Bear dye, and that makes macaroons grin, and that makes everybody miserable *just like me!*"

"I've figured it out!" cried Captain Jack, snapping his fingers. "I know exactly where I've seen that particular shade of green before!"

Now most of the bears turned from Boris to listen to Captain Jack, and Boris didn't like it one little bit.

"You listenick to *me,* bears!" he shouted.

"Where did you see it, Captain Jack?" asked Harry.

"I saw it in Lower South Blastok on a tree sloth," said Captain Jack. "The green color is caused by a completely harmless moss which grows in animal fur and can be easily removed by one or two applications of witch hazel."

Boris paused, and for the first time he looked really interested in what Captain Jack was saying.

"Vitch hazel? You sure what you're sayink is true?"
he asked Captain Jack.

"Absolutely," Captain Jack answered him. "That
green moss color is unmistakable, and I guaranty you
can have it completely cleared up in a couple of days."

Boris spread his arms in disgust.

"Vitch hazel! Why didn't someone tellink me this
before?" he cried.

Sometime later, when they had gotten Boris calmed
down with some witch hazel and taken him to the
courthouse to see what the law would do to him, which
probably wouldn't be much as it was obvious his turning green had upset him terribly and probably not made
him entirely responsible for his actions, a happy moment came to the National Macaroon Factory. For the
first time in months a batch of macaroons came off the
production line without a single, tiny trace of green in
them! They were, one and all, a lovely golden color just
like macaroons ought to be!

"Oh, I'm so happy, Harry!" cried dear old Mrs.
Sweetly, dabbing at her eyes with a small hankie. "And
it's all because of you!"

"That's true, Harry," said Fred.

"Without you, my boy," added Captain Jack, "this affair would probably never have been cleared up, and I wouldn't have found out about spectacles."

Harry cleared his throat, not used to having all this fuss made over him, but he was very pleased.

"Here, Harry," said Mrs. Sweetly, taking the first of the fresh, new macaroons from the production line and handing it to the fat bear spy, "I think you should be the one to eat this."

And Harry did, and it was very, very good.

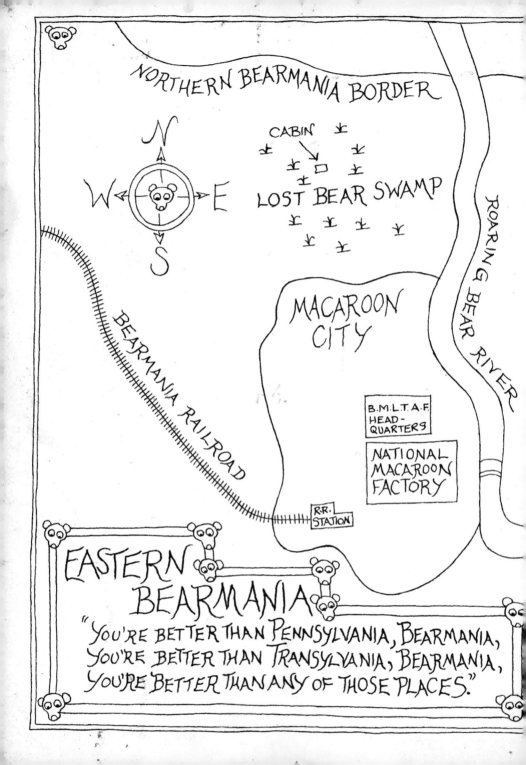